SCARE SCHOOL
~Diaries~
Forest Frights

SCARE SCHOOL Diaries

Forest Frights

BY JARRETT LERNER

ALADDIN
New York   London   Toronto   Sydney   New Delhi

For Supriya

If you purchased this book without a cover, you should be aware that this book is stolen property. It was reported as "unsold and destroyed" to the publisher, and neither the author nor the publisher has received any payment for this "stripped book."

This book is a work of fiction. Any references to historical events, real people, or real places are used fictitiously. Other names, characters, places, and events are products of the author's imagination, and any resemblance to actual events or places or persons, living or dead, is entirely coincidental

ALADDIN
An imprint of Simon & Schuster Children's Publishing Division
1230 Avenue of the Americas, New York, New York 10020
First Aladdin paperback edition November 2024
Copyright © 2024 by Jarrett Lerner
Also available in an Aladdin hardcover edition.
All rights reserved, including the right of reproduction in whole or in part in any form.
ALADDIN and related logo are registered trademarks of Simon & Schuster, LLC.
Simon & Schuster: Celebrating 100 Years of Publishing in 2024
For information about special discounts for bulk purchases, please contact Simon & Schuster Special Sales at 1-866-506-1949 or business@simonandschuster.com.
The Simon & Schuster Speakers Bureau can bring authors to your live event. For more information or to book an event contact the Simon & Schuster Speakers Bureau at 1-866-248-3049 or visit our website at www.simonspeakers.com.
Designed by Irene Vandervoort
The illustrations for this book were rendered digitally.
The text of this book was set in Scare School Thick.
Manufactured in the United States of America 0924 OFF
2 4 6 8 10 9 7 5 3
Library of Congress Cataloging-in-Publication Data
Names: Lerner, Jarrett, author, illustrator.
Title: Forest frights / Jarrett Lerner.
Description: First Aladdin hardcover/paperback edition. | New York : Aladdin, 2024. | Audience: Ages 5 to 8. | Summary: It is his second year of Scare School for Bash the ghost, and when he is paired with Vlad and Vicky, the mischievous vampires, he is worried that their antics will sabotage their group project.
Identifiers: LCCN 2024017663 (print) | LCCN 2024017664 (ebook) | ISBN 9781665922111 (pbk) | ISBN 9781665922128 (hc) | ISBN 9781665922135 (ebook)
Subjects: LCSH: Ghost stories. | Vampires—Juvenile fiction. | Schools—Juvenile fiction. | Forests and forestry—Juvenile fiction. | Fear—Juvenile fiction. | CYAC: Ghosts—Fiction. | Vampires—Fiction. | Schools—Fiction. | Forests and forestry—Fiction. | Fear—Fiction. | LCGFT: Picture books.
Classification: LCC PZ7.1.L4685 Fo 2024 (print) | LCC PZ7.1.L4685 (ebook) | DDC 813.6 [E]—dc23/eng/20240520
LC record available at https://lccn.loc.gov/2024017663
LC ebook record available at https://lccn.loc.gov/2024017664

For Bash's eyes
ONLY

DO NOT TURN ANOTHER PAGE

I'm watching you...

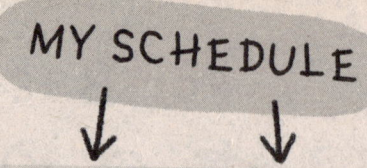

Student: Bash (ghost)
Homeroom: Graves

Period	Class
1	Introduction to Scare Tactics with Ms. Graves
2	Cackles, Laughs, and other Sinister Sounds with Mr. Crane
3	Human Behavior with Headmaster Dave
4	Lunch with Captain Loosebeard
5	Advanced Creeping and Crawling with Prof. Snekk
6	Philosophy of Fear with Ms. Scully
7	Creature Intensive with Mr. Crane

Sunday

Tomorrow morning, I get to go back to Scare School!

It's funny. Just a couple of weeks ago, I was TERRIFIED to go to Scare School for the first time. But now I can't wait to hurry up and get back.

This happened yesterday morning.

As excited as I am to get back to Scare School, I WILL miss Dad once I'm there. We had an awesome weekend together.

Dad (actually super cool)

Tonight, for my last night home, Dad made me a special dinner. It was sort of like what he cooked a couple of weeks ago—a meal of all my favorite things. Pizza. Peppers. And Popsicles.

But this time, Dad decided to COMBINE all three things. His idea, he said, was to make a "Super Letter-P Pizza." But then he got a little carried away and started adding a bunch more stuff that started with the letter p. Like pretzels. And pecans. And pears. And peas.

It tasted . . . interesting. The peppers, pears, and peas were all delicious mixed with the cheese and tomato sauce. And the pretzels were actually pretty good too. But the pecans were a little weird. And the Popsicles? Those melted as soon as Dad stuck the pizza in the oven, obviously. Then the juice from the things gave the whole pie this bright pinkish tint.

And then there was the problem of the sticks. . . .

Anyway, it's gotten late. And the sooner I go to bed, the sooner I'll wake up tomorrow and be able to get on my way back to Scare School.

So, you know:

GOOD NIGHT!

Monday

My first day back at Scare School was . . . interesting. Just like Dad's Super Letter-P Pizza.

I think I'll tell you about the GOOD stuff before I tell you about the NOT-SO-GOOD stuff. I'll start at the beginning. . . .

Dad and I got up bright and early and hit the road. Last time it'd taken us forty-five minutes to fly to Scare School. But I guess because I'd been so nervous about actually GETTING there, I'd gone pretty slow.

LAST TIME

This time, I led the way—and we shaved seven minutes off our flight!

THIS TIME

We zipped around the spooky forest outside the school, and just as we left the last of the trees behind, I spotted it.

A big grin spread across my face. And then I really started flying.

The school's big front door was wide open, and Headmaster Dave was there greeting everyone.

I paused long enough to say hello, then raced inside. And right there, hanging out in the school's entryway, were all my friends and favorite teachers.

Itsy

Batslee

Captain Loosebeard

Mimi

Ms. Scully

There were some OTHER creatures there, too....

Vlad

Mr. Crane

Vicky

But I just focused on my pals.

I flew over to Itsy, and everything I'd been saving up to tell her all weekend came bursting out of me. And apparently SHE had been saving up a ton of stuff to tell me, too.

Oh! One other cool thing that happened:

Wes came over while Itsy and I were catching up. He had his whole family with him. One of his parents had their hand on Wes's back, almost like he'd needed a push to come over to me and Itsy.

And Wes's older brother—he had a hand on Wes's shoulder. Just gently, though. Sort of like he was trying to remind his little brother that he was there.

I noticed all this before I saw what Wes was holding.

SKETCHBOOKS!

"Wes!" I said. "Are those your sketchbooks?"

At first, Wes didn't answer. Then his brother gave his shoulder a little squeeze and he said,

Um, ah, yeah. I—I, uh... I thought, maybe, if you wanted to, if you weren't busy sometime, maybe... you'd want to see?

I grinned. Then I said,

Wes? That is the silliest question ever asked in the history of the world. Ever.

Wes's parents laughed. So did his brother. And it was a little hard to tell because of all the hair on his face, but I'm pretty sure that Wes was grinning, too.

Two seconds later Headmaster Dave announced that it was time to say goodbye to our families and get our day started.

Just before I headed over to Dad, I saw Wes's brother give him a high five and say, "See, bro? I knew you could do it."

I found Dad on the other side of the entryway with Mimi's mom. And as excited as I was to be back at Scare School, it wasn't easy saying bye to him. I wouldn't see him again until NEXT Friday.

That's ELEVEN whole days.

TODAY

WHEN I SEE DAD AGAIN!

Dad gave me a hug, then flew off—and that's when things started going downhill. . . .

Headmaster Dave said that he was glad to have us back, then told us that we'd be spending much of our second two-week session at Scare School working on a group project.

I should say, I was actually happy to hear this part of things. Last session I'd had to pass my C.A.T., which stands for Creature Aptitude Test. Itsy had helped me prepare for the test—but I'd had to pass it all on my own. And it had been TOUGH.

So a group project?

That sounded GREAT.

Don't they say two heads are better than one? And a group can have three or four heads.

Or five!

Speaking of heads, right after I started thinking all this, Headmaster Dave said,

When I heard the word "pick," I thought Headmaster Dave meant that WE would be doing the picking. And I knew who I'd pick first. Itsy, of course. Followed by Mimi. And then Batslee and Wes.

But then Captain Loosebeard cleared his throat. I turned to look at him and saw that he was holding a big bowl full of little slips of paper.

Almost as scary as a bowl of Captain Loosebeard's Bean Surprise!

Uh-oh.

WE weren't going to be picking our groups—HE was.

And I don't think I can stand to go through it all over again, so I'm just going to come right out and say it:

First I got paired with Wes. Which was EXCELLENT.

But the next two names that Captain Loosebeard pulled out of his bowl?

They were VLAD and VICKY. In other words, the OPPOSITE of excellent.

It's going to be a long eleven days....

Tuesday

Have I mentioned before how amazing Itsy is?

BEST best friend in the whole entire universe

(Just kidding—I know I did a whole bunch in my last notebook.)

This morning, she TOTALLY saved me.

I guess, after being home for a bit, I got used to sleeping in again.

But today was our first day back having classes, and our classes start EARLY.

So there I was, snoozing away. And I probably would've kept right on snoring until third or fourth period if Itsy hadn't woken me up.

First period, we have Introduction to Scare Tactics with Ms. Graves.

This session of your studies is one of my absolute favorites.

She went on to tell us that we were going to learn about some ways to make ourselves look extra frightening, and also how to use darkness to our advantage.

It sounded cool (but also, if I'm being honest, a little scary... I'm not the biggest fan of the dark.)

But before we could get to all THAT, Ms. Graves said we first had to talk about our...

GROUP PROJECT!

When I heard those words, I felt two things at once—one of them good, one of them bad.

The good feeling I had was about Wes, obviously.

I'm psyched I get to spend a bunch of time with him during these next two weeks of school. I think we could be really great friends.

And the BAD feeling I had?

I probably don't even need to say it...

But it was about THESE two:

Ugh.

Anyway, Ms. Graves explained that our group project was a RESEARCH project. We had to pick a place in or around Scare School, read all about it, then write up a report sharing everything we'd learned.

Then Ms. Graves handed out a list of the places we could choose from.

1. Basement
2. Attic
3. Forest
4. Classroom 14B

I kind of wished Ms. Graves would've just picked a place FOR us. I mean, I didn't really want to explore ANY of them, so I wasn't sure how we'd choose.

But Ms. Graves said that a big part of our grade on the project was going to be how well we worked together. And the first test of our team was making a group decision.

It all turned out to be even harder than I thought....

At lunch, Wes and I went to talk to Vlad and Vicky. We asked them if they wanted to meet up after classes to pick our place and then maybe go to the library to find some books about it.

And Vlad said, "Maybe."

We told the vampires we'd be in the library right after classes— if, you know, it turned out they weren't too busy.

But they didn't show up.

Wes and I sat there waiting for a while. Then we finally gave up and left.

On our way back to our rooms, we found out what it was that Vlad and Vicky were "busy" with. They were in the gym, just kicking around a ball!

I couldn't believe it! They weren't busy at all!

Nope.

They are NOT.

Wednesday

Last night Itsy told me that HER group already picked a place for their project. (They chose the basement.) They even went to library and found a bunch of books!

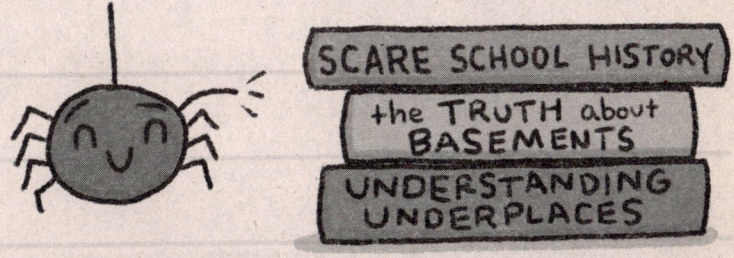

At lunch Wes and I went over to Vlad and Vicky again. But this time, instead of asking if they wanted to meet LATER, we just took a seat, forcing them to have a meeting right there and then.

Since Itsy's group had already chosen the basement, we only had three options left: the attic, the forest, or classroom 14B.

I REALLY didn't want to do classroom 14B. I don't even like flying past the place....

So I said,

But Vlad said,

So I said,

> Oh-KAY. Then how about the forest?

But Vlad said,

> Not a good idea.

> I'M allergic to most trees.

And even though I really didn't even want to suggest it, I was so frustrated that I shouted out,

But Vlad said,

I was ready to EXPLODE.

Before I could, though, Vlad finally gave in. He sighed and said,

Fine. We'll do the forest. Whatever.

Wes told the vampires we'd be in the library after classes again. Hopefully, I added, they wouldn't be too busy to join us. Then Wes and I left.

And—surprise, surprise—Vlad and Vicky didn't show up this afternoon, either.

But Wes and I did find a bunch of books for us to use.

After we checked out all the books, Wes started packing up his backpack like he was getting ready to leave.

I was watching him, and so I caught a glimpse of his sketchbooks—the same ones he'd shown me the other day when we'd all gotten back to school.

"Your sketchbooks," I said.

"Oh." Wes froze, sort of like he'd forgotten his sketchbooks were even in there. "Yeah."

"Did you . . . ," I said. I was careful, because I know how hard it is for ME to share my art with other people. "Did you still want to show me some of your drawings?"

And even though I couldn't see his face—you know, because of all the hair—I could tell he was nervous. It was something about how his back had gotten hunched and his shoulders had sunk.

"I mean...," Wes said. "If you really..."

I was about to promise him that I really DID want to see his art. Before I could, though, he said something else. But quietly, like he was just saying it to himself, so I only heard some of the words.

I will not ... fears ...
me back.

All of a sudden, then, Wes sat up. He pulled all his sketchbooks out of his backpack, set them on the table, and slid them over toward me.

I looked.

And I looked and looked and looked some more.

I probably could've gone on looking all day—and maybe even all night, too.

Wes is an AMAZING artist.

I mean, I knew that already, since I'd gotten a couple glimpses of Wes's drawings during last session.

But getting to just sit there and flip through his sketchbooks—well, NOW I knew that he was AMAZINGLY AMAZING.

And seeing his artwork?

It made my brain buzz, and gave me all kinds of ideas for my own drawings that I'd never had before.

Anyway, at dinner tonight I told Itsy all about Wes's sketchbooks. I even looked around for the werewolf—I wanted to ask him if he'd show them to Itsy, too. He must have eaten earlier, though, because I couldn't find him in the cafeteria.

Then something knocked all that out of my head. Ms. Scully came around with the day's mail— and there was a letter for me.

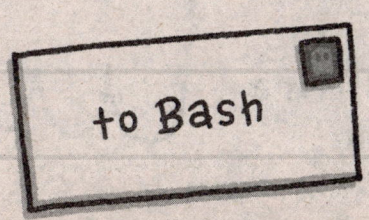
to Bash

I could tell by the handwriting on the envelope that it was from my sister.

Bella (my big sister)

not my biggest fan (though has been kind of nice to me since I started at Scare School)

INCREDIBLE (and I mean INCREDIBLE) at ghost stuff

already has a really good job haunting a whole entire house

What's up, little bro?

Dad told me you passed your big test. Nice work. Maybe you're not so terrible at being a ghost, after all. Either that or you just got lucky. Ha.

If I remember right, you do a group project during the second session of Scare School. Did I ever tell you about that? My group did the forest, and one night, I went in there and gathered up a ton of razor-toothed snarl blossoms. I brought them to our presentation, and they were just hissing and spitting at everyone.

It was EPIC.

Don't worry — I went back to the forest later on and replanted the little guys. They were fine. Just a little terrified.

Speaking of terrified, I should probably get back to work. This house isn't going to haunt itself.

Good luck on your project.

I hope you get a good group. That's pretty much half the battle.

— Bella

Great.

As if the situation weren't bad enough, now all the teachers are going to compare my project to my brilliant big sister's.

Maybe we really should have picked classroom 14B.

Thursday

Last night I barely slept. Bella's letter had gotten me even more worried about our group project, and I just couldn't quiet down my brain enough to really get any rest.

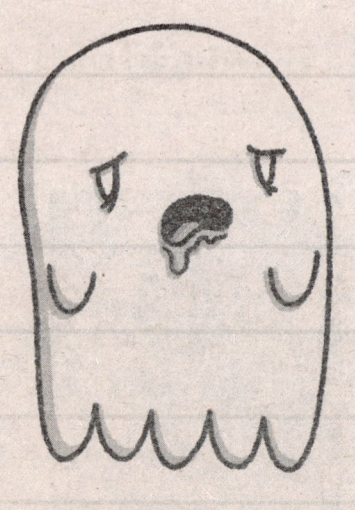

Me, when Itsy (again) woke me up this morning

Even though I was exhausted, Itsy and I somehow made it to first period a couple of minutes early. Waiting for class to get going, I actually started to (finally!) drift off to sleep.

But Ms. Graves took care of that. She slipped into the room without any of us noticing, then got class started with a BANG.

Or I guess I should say a BOO....

Once we had all calmed down, Ms. Graves explained that her BOO was part of our day's lesson.

She had scared us, she said, thanks to the "element of surprise." Then she went up to the board and started a list.

1. SURPRISE

"Surprise," Ms. Graves told us, was the first of three Scare Tactics we were going to be studying.

The other two?

> 1. SURPRISE
> 2. SIZE
> 3. SHADOW

I got out a piece of paper to take some notes—and that's when my sleepy brain all of a sudden perked up with a thought.

As soon as class ended, I flew over to Wes and told him all about it.

We had to wait until lunch to see if my idea would actually work. And unfortunately I had two more classes before it was lunchtime.

THIRD PERIOD

Human Behavior with Headmaster Dave

Finally it was lunch, and Wes and I didn't waste any time putting the plan we made earlier into action. We met up at the table where Itsy and I always sit—and then we went over to where Vlad and Vicky were. They noticed us just before we reached them. And when they looked up, Wes and I both shouted,

SURPRISE!

We quickly sat down across from the vampires. Then Wes reached into his backpack and pulled out the books that we'd gotten from the library yesterday. It all happened so fast, Vicky and Vlad didn't even have time to react.

That was as far as MY idea took us. But then Wes jumped in.

Well, first he did that thing— the same thing he did the day before in the library. He muttered something to himself. I couldn't hear it all this time either. It was too noisy in the cafeteria. But I could hear enough to know that it was the same thing he'd told himself last time.

...will not let... fears... hold me...

After that, Wes moved the books around so there was one in front of each of us. He said we needed to start reading them right away, and that we should try to finish them by the end of the weekend.

I thought Vlad and Vicky were going to make a fuss about this. Neither of them really seemed to like reading or doing schoolwork. And they REALLY didn't seem to like other people—especially other KIDS—telling them what to do.

But I think they were so surprised by the way Wes had taken charge, they forgot to get upset and argue with him. They just sat there, clutching their books and gaping at him.

And speaking of surprises, Wes finally said something that even I couldn't help but make a fuss about:

Wes said that he thought our project would be way better if we had "firsthand experience" of what the forest was like.

Which makes sense, I guess.

But I couldn't help staring at the cover of the book Wes had given me, and feeling like it maybe wasn't worth it.

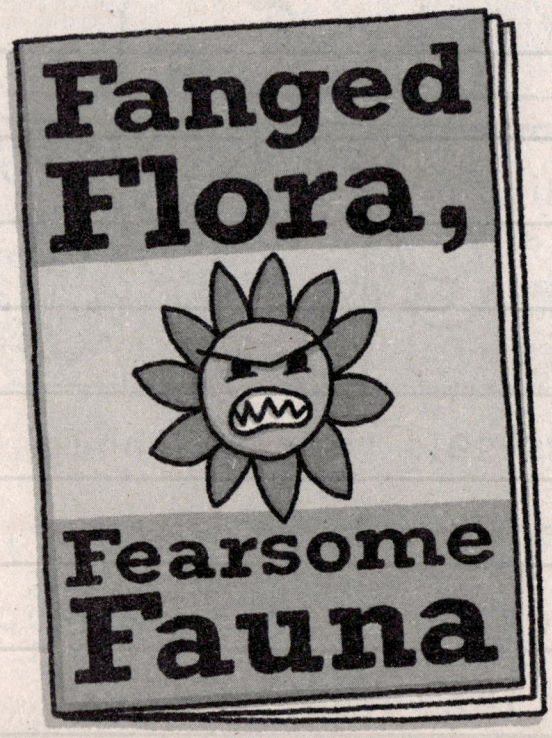

I mean, I know Bella went in there and got back out just fine. But Bella is BELLA. And I'm ME.

Bella (again)

I know I already said that she's INCREDIBLE at ghost stuff, but did I mention how brave (and bold and daring and unfazed and unafraid and NOT SCARED OF ANYTHING AT ALL EVER) she is???

Based on the looks on their faces, Vlad and Vicky didn't seem too happy about the idea of going into the forest either. And I think Vlad was about two seconds away from arguing with Wes about it. But before he could say a word, Wes stood up.

And with that, Wes turned around and left.

Then, believe it or not, I was surprised all over again.

FIFTH PERIOD

Advanced Creeping and Crawling with Professor Snekk

"Snekk snekk snekk snekk..."

SIXTH PERIOD

Philosophy of Fear with Ms. Scully

"Fear is commonly accompanied by other emotions."

"Embarrassment, for instance. Even shame."

SEVENTH PERIOD

Creature Intensive with Mr. Crane

Okay, Bash. Let's practice your invisibility again.

Good...

Good...

Good...

Not THAT good.

Friday

I really, really, REALLY wish we hadn't chosen to do our project on the forest.

One reason is because I spent yesterday afternoon reading some of my book about it. And it turns out that those creatures on the cover aren't even the scariest ones in there. Not even close!

Also, I told Itsy about Wes's plan for us to go check out the forest for ourselves. And guess what?! HER group had planned to do the same thing for THEIR project—to take a trip down to the Scare School basement—but Headmaster Dave told them they COULDN'T. He said the place was "way too dangerous."

So at dinner last night, I told Headmaster Dave about OUR plan to visit the forest. But he didn't react like I hoped he would.

Fun?

FUN?!

Yeah, right.

I spent my morning classes trying to figure out how to get out of actually going into the forest. I thought about saying I was allergic to most trees, like Vlad had told us the other day.

But that wasn't true, and I didn't really want to lie to Wes. We had just started becoming better friends, and I was super excited about that. Lying to him seemed like a great way to mess that all up.

On my way to the cafeteria for lunch, I flew by Vicky and Vlad in the hallway. They were leaning close to each other, in the middle of what looked like an intense conversation. So intense, they didn't even notice me.

I couldn't be sure. But it kind of sounded like they were talking about going into the forest. And Vlad? He sounded nervous about it. As nervous as I was.

I assumed it was because of his allergies. And then, because I didn't want them to catch me listening in, I flew off. I went the long way around the school and to the cafeteria.

At lunch, Wes confirmed our afternoon plans.

So I'll see you at the front entrance after seventh period?

Since I hadn't come up with a way to wriggle out of going, I just gulped and gave Wes a nod.

And after seventh period, I told Itsy to wish me luck, and then I headed to the front of the school.

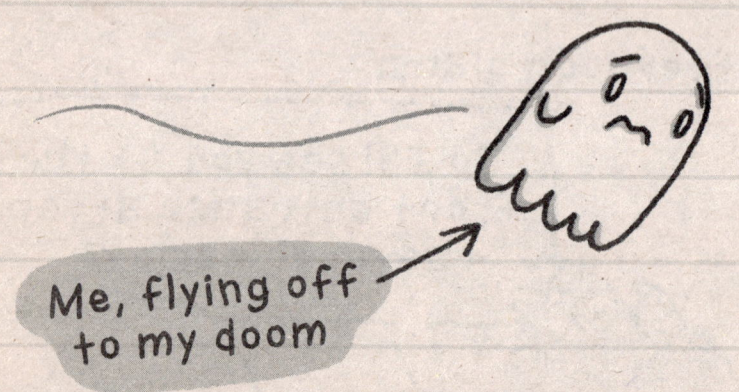

Me, flying off to my doom

Wes was already there when I arrived. Vlad and Vicky were NOT.

But seventh period had only just ended, so we decided to give them a few more minutes.

FIVE MINUTES LATER

FIVE MORE MINUTES LATER

YET ANOTHER FIVE MINUTES LATER

Eventually Wes said, "This is ridiculous."

Then he took a deep breath, turned around, and shoved open the front door.

Out we went.

Wes walked FAST, and took a bunch more deep breaths as we headed toward the forest.

"Maybe..." I said, hurrying to keep up with him. "Maybe Vlad's allergies are really bad."

Wes shook his head and kept on stomping toward the forest.

By the time we got there, he seemed to have calmed down some.

He paused to take one more breath. Then, without any warning, he plunged into the forest. I swear, I just blinked— and all of a sudden he'd totally disappeared into the shadows between the trees.

Uhhh, Wes?

He didn't say a thing.
Until he did.

Which, obviously, is the VERY LAST THING you want to hear your friend say right after they plunge into a dark forest.

I swung a little closer to the trees.

"Quick! Come look!" Wes called out to me.

Weirdly, he didn't sound scared, like he would have if he'd been cornered by a pair of razor-toothed snarl blossoms. He just sounded... disappointed.

So I flew in, between the same two trees Wes had walked through.

I almost bumped right into him.

I looked.

But there was nothing to look AT.

There were no razor-toothed snarl blossoms or stupefying ferns. There were no man-eating mega flies or slime-spewing behemoth beetles.

There were just lots of trees, plus a whole bunch of plain old, not-at-all-scary leaves.

Wes said, "I can't believe it."

And I couldn't either.

I'd been so worried, but it turned out the forest wasn't scary at all!

Or so I thought....

Because then Wes said, "Wait a second. OF COURSE the plants and creatures aren't out yet. They only come out at night!"

He did.

But only because he wanted to make a plan to return to the forest later, at night—and also a plan to make sure Vlad and Vicky joined us.

Saturday

Yesterday afternoon, after our uneventful trip into the forest, Wes and I couldn't find Vlad or Vicky anywhere. The vampires didn't even show up for dinner. They weren't at breakfast this morning, either.

It was a rainy morning, meaning all the outdoor activities the teachers had planned for us got postponed. So Ms. Scully and Captain Loosebeard opened up the gym, and told everyone that they could play and hang out in there.

But Itsy and I decided to head to the library and—finally—get to work on our comic. We'd been planning to make one since the week before, but hadn't had much time to actually do it. Pretty much all we'd done was come up with our two main characters.

"Okay," Itsy said once we got settled in the library. "If we want to make a full-on comic, we'll need a bad guy."

We sat there and brainstormed for a minute.

All of a sudden the creatures from the book about the forest I'd been reading popped into my head.

I told Itsy my idea.

And guess what?

She loved it!

So we got to work.

We drew, wrote, and discussed story ideas until lunchtime. Then we packed up our stuff and headed to the cafeteria.

Pretty much the second I flew in, Wes called out to me.

When I went over, Wes said, "Quick! Before they leave."

The next thing I knew, I was hurrying after him—and heading directly for the table where Vlad and Vicky were sitting, eating their lunch.

I don't know if Wes took any deep breaths on his way over to them. And I also don't know if he muttered those same words to himself—the ones about not letting his fears hold him back. Because by the time I caught up to him, he was already talking to the vampires.

It took a few seconds, but eventually, Vlad and Vicky both shook their heads.

Wes told Vicky and Vlad about how we'd gone into the forest the day before, but how none of the plants or creatures were out yet. He said that the only way we could do any actual RESEARCH was if we went in at night.

Well... well I can't go tonight.

Why not?

Wes was getting SERIOUSLY frustrated. I thought he might tear his hair out—ALL of it.

But he just said, "Fine. WEDNESDAY night." And before Vlad could make an excuse about why he couldn't go then, he added, "We HAVE to go then. We'll need Thursday to DO the project."

Vlad didn't say anything right away. But then—FINALLY—he said,

After which he and Vicky went back to their lunches.

Wes glared at the vampires for a second longer.

Then we left.

Monday

It rained again yesterday, so Itsy and I spent another day in the library, working on our comic. I was going to invite Wes to join us, but I didn't see him at breakfast, and then Itsy and I got so carried away with what we were doing, we totally missed lunch!

We had run into a bit of a problem: we now had plenty of bad guys for our superheroes to battle, but we didn't know what the bad guys should actually DO. We came up with a bunch of ideas, but none of them really excited us all that much.

I went to bed wondering about it, and woke up this morning wondering about it too.

But then it was time for class.

And Ms. Graves had another trick up her sleeve.

The period had already started— but she was nowhere in sight.

Someone had turned out the lights!

But they were only out for a second.

When they came back on, there was . . . something at the front of the room. A big, shadowy SOMETHING.

Suddenly, the big, shadowy SOMETHING at the front of the room began to laugh. The laugh sounded a lot like Ms. Graves. Because it WAS Ms. Graves! The whole entire time!

Surprise. Size. And Shadow. Our three Scare Tactics at work.

Then she said, "Today, we'll be discussing how these techniques can be used to scare others, and also how they are often used by creatures who are scared THEMSELVES. Out in the wild, you will frequently find the Scare Tactics being employed as a means of DEFENSE."

For some reason, when Ms. Graves said this, I thought about the letter Bella had sent me. About how she'd said those razor-toothed snarl blossoms she'd brought to her group project presentation had been "terrified." And then I had one of those things that Itsy had explained to me during our first session of Scare School: an EPIPHANY.

Me, all of a sudden realizing something

Tuesday

Today, every single one of our teachers brought up the group project.

It wasn't easy hearing all this, especially since my group was so far behind.

And outside class, it wasn't like I got a break from thinking about it.

This happened after classes...

I know Itsy wasn't trying to make me feel bad or anything.

But I still changed the subject as quickly as I could.

Hey, um... Want to work on our comic?

Oh! Speaking of our comic—I never told you anything about the idea I had for it in class yesterday.

But why TELL you about it when I can just SHOW you.

Drumroll please...

That's a draft of a cover for Itsy's and my first comic.

We still don't have a title.

But we're going to try to think of one before bed tonight. IF, that is, Itsy can stop talking about the basement....

OH! I can't believe I didn't tell you THIS! The basement...

Wednesday

Well, it's official: today was the longest—and also the STRANGEST—day of my life.

Also probably the most exhausting.

But, if I go to bed now, I'm worried that I'll forget some stuff I want to get down here. So I'm going to stay up just a little longer. Hopefully I don't fall asleep in the middle of a sentence.

ZZZZZZ...

Anyway, the first half of the day actually went by really slowly. I was eager to just hurry up and get to the end of it so that Wes and Vlad and Vicky and I could finally get into the forest—and then, IF we managed to get back out again, get to work on our project.

The later it got, though, the more I remembered what we were going to SEE in the forest.

And it was THEN that the day started going by FAST.

At dinner, Wes told me when and where to meet. He also said he'd already let Vlad and Vicky know.

When I said I'd see them there, Vlad said, "Maybe you will, maybe you won't."

Later, back in our room, Itsy got ready for bed.

Itsy's cozy socks she sleeps in (she knit them herself!)

Then she crawled into bed with a book.

It was weird not getting into bed too. And even weirder, later on, when I left our room and went to meet Wes, Vicky, and Vlad.

When I turned the corner, I was glad to see that everyone was already there—Vlad included. He was standing a little ways away from Wes and Vicky, and sort of hunching over and holding his stomach. But he was there!

For some reason, though, Wes still looked unhappy.

I looked at Vlad. Then I took a deep breath. Because I'd prepared for this moment. I knew what I had to do...

First of all, I flew over to the vampire. And on the way, I gave myself a bit of a pep talk. Because what I was about to do? It wasn't going to be easy.

I kept my voice low, so Wes and Vicky couldn't hear me, and I said, "The forest at night sounds pretty scary, huh?"

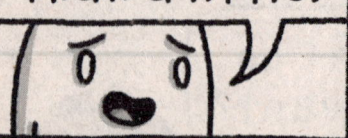

Vlad didn't say anything for several seconds. He just looked at me, and seemed to be seriously thinking over everything I'd said. Then, finally...

Wes and Vicky watched him go. Then they both turned to me. They looked stunned.

And then it was MY turn to be stunned.

Because before she went after her brother, Vicky told me,

Once she was out the door, Wes said,

I knew what he meant.

Then we went. And I hadn't been lying to Vlad. Flying over to the forest, heading into the trees, I really WAS scared. But way less than I had been the other day. I think it was because I'd JUST done something scary—talking to Vlad like I had—and it had turned out totally fine. And believe it or not, it was the same with the forest. Not long after we all got in there, I started to realize that more than anything . . .

...the place was just AWESOME. The creatures and plants used all the usual scare tactics on us.

But, I now understood, this was only because THEY were scared too. Scared of US.

We all moved slowly, kept our hands in sight, and smiled, all to show we were friendly. And once the creatures and plants realized we weren't going to hurt them or steal their food, they dropped the act. And then they were just plain old COOL-looking. Some of them were also kind of cute.

We stayed in the woods for more than an hour, taking notes and making sketches whenever we got to a spot where there was enough moonlight to see our notebooks. Then we headed back to school.

Before we went our separate ways, we made a plan to spend tomorrow afternoon completing our project. It was going to be a ton of work. But for the first time since we'd got started, I really thought we could all do it.

Then Vlad hung back a second, even after his sister had gone off.

He turned around to go.

I stopped him just as he was turning the corner.

Okay.

Now I really need to go to bed.

After all, I've got a project to help finish tomorrow.

Thursday

Remember last night, when I said that yesterday was probably the most exhausting day of my life?

I was wrong. TODAY was the most exhausting day of my life.

Most of our teachers gave us their class periods to work on our projects, which was great. (Can you guess which teacher DIDN'T? Here's a hint: his name rhymes with Mr. Train. . . .)

Here's another hint: he looks like this.

Even so, Wes and Vlad and Vicky and I still had to work all afternoon and evening to finish up the main part of our project. Then, after dinner, we each went back to our own rooms to put the final touches on a few last things.

I was in charge of the project's cover. Pretty cool, right?

Anyway, it's late.

Itsy's asleep, and has been for a while.

And tomorrow morning, I've got a pretty important project to help present.

So, you know:

GOOD NIGHT!

Friday

This morning there were no normal classes. Instead we all gathered in the cafeteria.

Captain Loosebeard had rearranged the tables so we could all sit together. He served us breakfast, and after we ate, it was time to present our projects.

Ms. Graves asked Itsy's group to go first. They did—and totally crushed it. They all made Scare School's basement sound so interesting that, if Headmaster Dave would've let us, I might have gone down there to check it out.

Also, Itsy drew a bunch of pictures for her project. They were awesome.

Next it was our turn.

We hadn't had much time the day before to practice the presentation part of the project, so we were a little all over the place in the beginning. But we pretty quickly sorted ourselves out, and then things actually went really well.

Ms. Graves was thrilled when we got to the part about the creatures and plants of the forest using the three Scare Tactics. And Ms. Scully gave me a big thumbs-up when I talked about how, a lot of the time, when we're scared of something, we make that thing seem even scarier in our heads than it really is.

Once we were done, we got a round of applause. Which felt great. And then Professor Snekk slithered over to me and said,

Snekk snekk snekk-snekk snekk. Snekk SNEKK snekk

Which felt . . . confusing.

But Captain Loosebeard helped me translate.

He said that you remind him of your sister.

Speaking of Bella, I wrote her a quick letter this afternoon, not long before Dad showed up to get me for the weekend. And there are just enough pages in this notebook for me to let you know what I said. (And now I need to go and get another notebook!)

Bella,

I made it through another session of Scare School! I don't know if I'm getting any better at being a ghost, but I AM learning things. AMAZING things. In class and outside of it.

This week, I learned that everyone—and I mean EVERYONE—is scared of something. Even vampires. Even Dad. Even Mr. Crane. Even YOU. And somehow, knowing THAT—it makes the whole world feel a little less scary.

— Bash